Animals Are out of th

by Verses for the Voiceless

ACKNOWLEDGEMENTS

This book would not have been possible without the help of these contributors:

Our Sponsor, Angela Stephens

Our Organization Head, Storey Wertheimer

Our Editor, Storey Wertheimer

Our Cover and Title Page Illustrator, Cassie Levy

And our incredibly talented authors and illustrators:

Abby Safier, Anique Wertheimer, Ava Baak, Carol Nobili, Cassie Levy, Claire Saguy, Drew Safier, Emelia Weir, Etaih Van Herdewerden, Makenna Susman, Marisol Torro, Maxwell Bross, Sara Weinberg, Stella Raymond, Storey Wertheimer, and Tiffany Hong

Illustated by: Drew Safier

Our Mission:

We are a group of high school students who are passionate about both creative writing and helping those in need. After doing research and finding that 2.5 million children in America are homeless, we could no longer stand on the sidelines. We started a project at our school called Verses for the Voiceless, in which we write poetry books designed for children of all ages. We donate 100% of the proceeds to charity organizations that design new futures for thousands of America's homeless youth.

Illustated by: Cassie Levy

PART 1:
ANIMALS GALORE!

Illustated by: Cassie Levy

Illustrated by: Abby Safier

Pets, Pets, Pets

Written by: Claire Saguy

Pets can be small
Enormous or tall
Sometimes with fur
Or nothing at all...

Some pets run fast
Like a cannon blast
Others are slow
They are always last

Some like to chew
On smelly brown boots
Other pets eat
Delicious fresh fruits

Some pets have fur
As dark as the night
And others have fur
As bright as sunlight

Some pets can fly
Across the blue sky

Some just have legs
And do not dare try!

Loud pets have barks
That echo through parks
While others can't be found
Cause they don't make a sound.

But when pets speak, each one
sounds unique
They purr and meow
Ruff and bow-wow
Squawk, squeak,
Croak or bleat

But no matter which pet you get
Big or small,
Short or tall,
Squawky or squeaky,
Croaky or bleaty,
They will love you with all their might
And hold you in their hearts oh so tight

The Animal Olympics
Written by: Anique Wertheimer
Illustrated by: Stella Raymond

It was 10 in the morning,
Things were getting tense,
Mr. Poodle up to bat,
It went out of the fence.

Mr. Bear was on the field,
Winning 4 goals to 1,
He had 7 goals,
By the time the game was done.

Baby Owl held the football,
Throwing 100 yards,
His throw went so far,
It almost hit the guards.

Larson the Fox stood there,
Scared as ever,
Could he beat that?
His answer was NEVER!

"Why did I even sign up?"
Is what Larson thought,
As he watched Rooster run,
His stomach tied up in a knot.

Larson walked to the exit,
But suddenly couldn't budge,
Grandpa Turtle stood before him,
"Larson!" He called with a nudge.

"Where are you going, old pal?
The game isn't even done.
I know you were meant for this,
There's no reason to run."

"I'm just not good!
Did you see Owl and Bear?
They were amazing,
The balls flew through the air!"

"Remember when you were little?
Always holding a ball?
Larson, you've been an athlete,
Before you could even crawl.

You haven't even tried,
Go back to the game,
You can't give up,
Or you'll be filled with shame."

"You're right, Grandpa!
I can't just walk away,
No matter whether I win,
I have a game to play!"

And sure enough,
Larson walked up to bat,
Put on his gloves,
His shin guards and hat.

He smashed the ball,
With all his might,
And it flew through the air,
With miraculous height!

He won the gold,
And Larson knew why,
Because Grandpa Turtle
encouraged him to try.

It was Grandpa he thanked,
For his wise advice,
That if you are going to give up,
You must pay a price.

A Tail and A Net

Written by: Carol Nobili and Storey Wertheimer

Illustrated by: Drew Safier

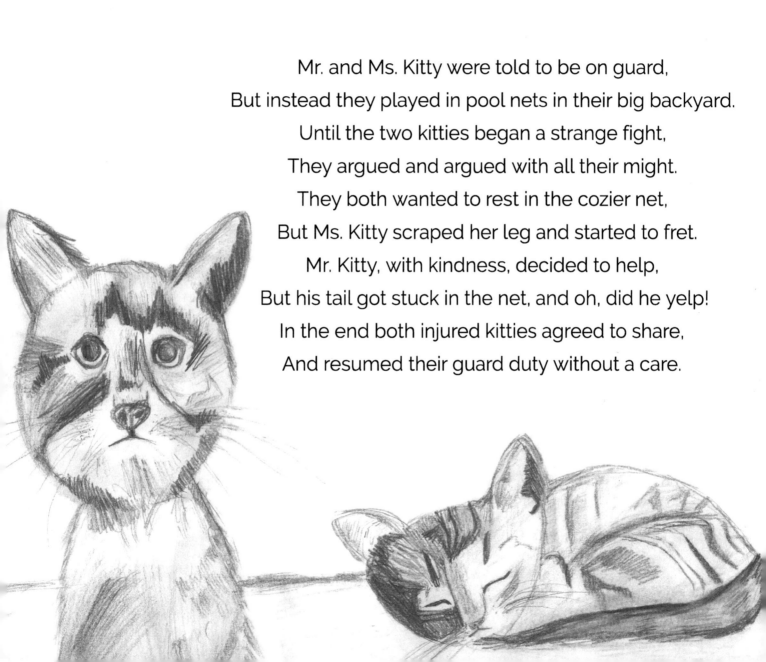

Mr. and Ms. Kitty were told to be on guard,

But instead they played in pool nets in their big backyard.

Until the two kitties began a strange fight,

They argued and argued with all their might.

They both wanted to rest in the cozier net,

But Ms. Kitty scraped her leg and started to fret.

Mr. Kitty, with kindness, decided to help,

But his tail got stuck in the net, and oh, did he yelp!

In the end both injured kitties agreed to share,

And resumed their guard duty without a care.

Cats

Written by: Carol Nobili

Illustrated by: Cassie Levy

Little cats, big cats
They are all so soft,
Even more fluffy
After they are washed
Usually friendly,
If handled gently.
They love to play,
Even when their toys are away.
If you carefully look into their eyes,
They sympathize.

A Year in the Life of Pets
Written by: Tiffany Hong
Illustrated by: Drew Safier

Spring:

Pets play in the rain

Muddy footprints everywhere

Oh no, it's filthy!

Summer:

Hiding and seeking

The sun gleams in the summer

Pets are delighted

Fall:

Pets play in the leaves

The big forests change colors

Hardly believing

Winter:

Foggy atmosphere

Bundled up in the winter

Pets shiver at night

Goldilocks

Written by: Marisol Torro

A flash of gold scales
Zip, zip, zap
The fish leaves a trail
Blurp, blurp, pop
With a swish of its tail

Where's the fish?
Gulp, gulp, stop
Behind the seaweed
fwish, fwish, peep
Look at that speed
As the fish finds its feed
The bright orange creature
is really a glee!

The Life of a Guppy

Written and Illustrated by:
Sara Weinberg

I am but a small fish in a fishbowl
Cramped alongside thirty other guppies
I pray to be rescued from this pet store prison
But why adopt a fish when next door are the
puppies?

Waldo McGee

Written by: Marisol Torro

Illustrated by: Cassie Levy

Where's my friend?
So many to choose
4 legs, 2 legs, no legs
It's a zoo!

A rabbit, no,
I don't think so
Maybe a frog?
But all it does is sit on a log.

I'd rather have a dog
But Mommy says, "no dog
for you,
I'll be the one scooping up
poo!"

A cat, a cat, a cat, a cat!
I want a kitty softer than a
hat.

One that purrs with delight
Oh a cat and I, we'll be a
sight.
It just feels right!

"No, no," Daddy says
"Cats make me sneeze and
wheeze
Then I can't breathe.
In a hotel I'll have to stay."

So I feel my hope slip away.
There's no pet for me.
I guess I 'll just buy a tree.

Wait, peep peep, what is
that sound?

Finally hopeful, I turn
around.

A bird, a chick! A yellow
puffball!
So sweet and gentle, not
too big at all,
A perfect companion just
for me!

Where's my friend?
Right here next to me
This is my chick,
Waldo McGee.

A Gift to Remember

Written and Illustrated by: Cassie Levy

Excitement filled my frame
Gift sat with ribbons on top
"I can't wait!" I exclaim
Ripping paper, my hands would not stop.
I tore the cardboard flaps
Eyes twinkled with disbelief
Out plopped a pup; hands clap!
Heart amazed beyond relief

Bird of Paradise

Written by: Maxwell Bross

Illustrated by: Cassie Levy

Bright colors gleam across the bright sky
As wings flap quickly through the big trees
The birds of paradise are flying high
Looking comfortable and at ease

Beautiful like moving masterpieces
Their caws keep traveling for miles
A parrot's beauty only increases
Bright colored patterns and complex styles

Puppies

Written by: Anique Wertheimer
Illustrated by: Abby Safier

They may be small,
Think they're strong like lions.
They may fall a lot,
But at least they're trying.
They may be confused,
But as cute as can be.
No matter what they eat,
They're always hungry.
They try to be good,
But they're usually not,
They try to be sneaky,
But always get caught.
They yip and yap
And bark and cry,
But we all love puppies,
Because we know they try.

Storms

Written by: Tiffany Hong
Illustrated by: Cassie Levy

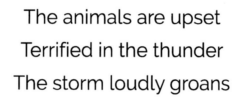

The animals are upset
Terrified in the thunder
The storm loudly groans

Illustrated by: Cassie Levy

Animals

Written by: Anique Wertheimer

Everyone loves animals
Sweet or goofy or cute,
They love the noises they make
From bark to meow to toot.

The deer is graceful and tall,
The elephant large and loud,
The bird can be so obnoxious
That it wakes up the whole crowd.

The cat is small and fluffy,
The dog happy and fun,
The bunny hips and hops
Until the day is done.

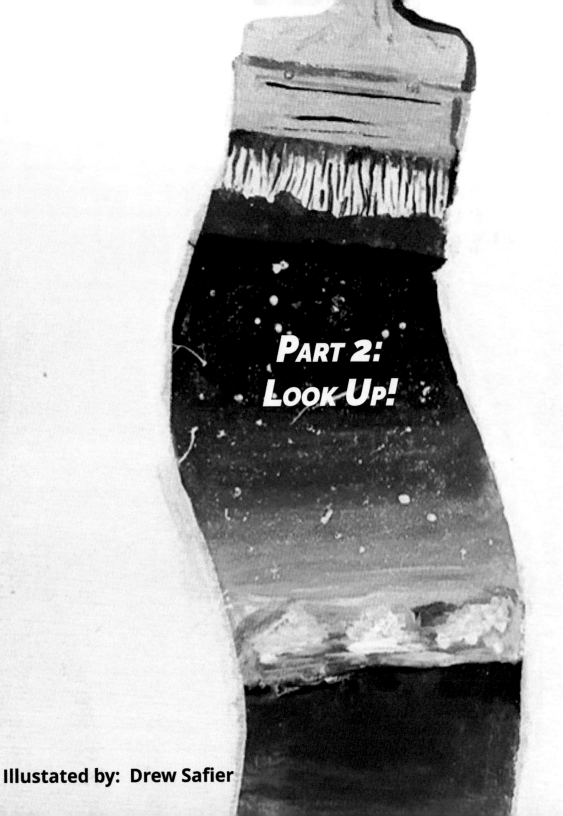

PART 2:
LOOK UP!

Illustated by: Drew Safier

Illustated by: Marisol Torro

Space Travel

Written by: Marisol Torro

Stars sprinkle the dark, endless sky

Planets spinning, glowing up high

Astronauts float in their little spaceships

Carefully avoiding all the asteroid bits

Even while speeding through space with a zip.

Illustated by: Etaih Van Herdewerden

LITTLE BROTHER

WRITTEN BY: SARA WEINBERG AND MAKENNA SUSMAN

No matter how big I get, I will always be the little brother,

If you want to know why then ask my mother.

My older brother is super cool

He makes the other constellations drool

Little Dipper is my name

I wish I could have some of my big brother's fame

In the endless night his kite loves to fly

But I wish I could be the constellation people easily spy.

Illustated by: Makenna Susman

My Pet Moon

Written by: Sara Weinberg and Makenna Susman

I love my pet moon with all of my heart

We are both funny, crazy and smart

At night we play hide and seek on the streets

But I am pretty sure my pet moon cheats

Wherever I go my pet moon is not far

My pet moon follows me in the car

Sadly the fun must wait until the sun goes down

Sharing the sky with the sun makes my pet moon frown

My pet moon at times seems really silly

But in the sky my pet moon gets pretty chilly

Some nights my pet moon has to wrap itself in a blankie

But not every night because the stars can get cranky

I will not settle for a dog or cat

My pet moon is perfect and I will leave it at that.

Illustated by: Makenna Susman

A Bad Case of Shapeshifting

Written by: Sara Weinberg and Makenna Susman

There is nothing I would rather do all day

Then float the day away

Up in the sky is where I feel free

I am a cloud and I am as happy as I can be

There is one small problem I forgot to mention

Something I should bring to your attention

As a cloud I cannot look in the mirror

The cause of which could not be any clearer

I can never tell what I look like

So I tell my reflection to take a hike

One minute you might think I am a giraffe eating a lollipop

The next I am a lady doing a bellyflop

Putting an end to my shape-shifting would be sweet

Seeing me for who I am would be a real treat.

Illustated by: Ava Baak

"Pluto Who?"
Written by: Sara Weinberg
and Makenna Susman

"Pluto is absent from class."

"Who is Pluto?", you might ask,

He is no longer allowed here

Nothing I do will make him appear

He is not a planet anymore

So his heart is feeling quite sore

He was just a bit too small

He could not reach the top of that wall!

So the mean people kicked him out,

Now Pluto must sit alone and pout.

"It's Me, Pluto"
Written by: Sara Weinberg
and Makenna Susman

Once upon a time I was a planet

But those days are over since I am no bigger than a pomegranate

I was never warned of the height rule

Judging planets by their size is quite cruel

I had to find myself a new crowd

It's the only place where us shorties are allowed

We are too short to be tall and too tall to be short

We are loved as much as a smelly wart

Dwarves are what they call us

That name really makes me fuss

I can't get my title back, no matter how hard I try

If I am not a planet, then what good am I?

The Star is Flying

Written by: Sara Weinberg and Makenna Susman

Illustrated by: Makenna Susman

I saw a star

Jump through the air

It was quite far

But I did not care

The bright light shot across the sky

I made a wish as it soared very high.

Outer Space

Written by: Carol Nobili

Illustrated by: Makenna Susman

Stars shine so bright in the sky,

They are the prettiest things passing by,

We can't touch them, but we watch them tower,

And everyone can feel their power,

The moon is like cheese, it's yellow and white,

Down it sheds a powerful light,

Every star is beautiful in its own way,

In the sky they will always stay,

It truly is an unreachable place,

Commonly known as outer space.

Stargazing

Written by: Carol Nobili

Many lights shine from the dark sky,

They are like sparks of hope dancing upon the eye,

No one has ever seen them shine like this before,

This is their time to truly roar,

Trust your instinct, when it comes from inside,

Follow the lights, and do not hide.

A slight hope will always remain,

Even when stars are blocked by gloomy rain.

It is remarkable what people near and far

Can gain from shooting for the stars.

Old Man Rainer's Words of Advice

Written by: Sara Weinberg and Makenna Susman

Illustrated by: Drew Safier

Diet: Do NOT try it!
I am Old Man Rainer of the sky
I see all with my little eye
Watching the humans is my treat
While I eat and eat and eat
All my food is neatly stacked in piles
I can eat all day, my stomach reaches for miles
One day I tried to go on a diet
But my stomach could not be quiet
Grumble Grumble, I really wonder
Why is it that humans call it thunder?
But the other day I just could not fit
In my chair when I really wanted to sit.

I wonder if it is possible for my belly to be even more round
These days it nearly touches the ground!
Oh no the tears are brimming
Watch out humans, you are going swimming!
Drop by drop my sad tears fall
I hold my fat tummy and begin to bawl
The world needs one giant drain
To soak up all of my rain
But I open my eyes and look down below
And I see all the plants that are starting to grow
If the Earth can be happy then so can I
There is nothing wrong with being a big guy!

Winter Wonderland

Written by: Storey Wertheimer

Illustrated by: Drew Safier

"Mommy, come here quick; look up at the sky!"
"Not again Joe. You point out enough planes passing by."
But this time, he was right- the weather was strange.
White flakes were falling, making the dirt's color suddenly change!

"Is the world coming to an end?"
"Come on now, Joe, please don't play pretend."
"Mommy for real, come over here."
At last she looked out. "It's snowing my dear!"

Joe had never seen a white flurry, for the sun usually shone
"Mommy, what is snow?" he asked in an excited tone.
"Put on a coat and some mittens, and I'll take you out!
We'll build a snowman. You'll love it, no doubt."

Together in Winter Wonderland they were able to play
Starting a snowball fight without any delay
"Mommy, pretty please, make it snow more!"
"I'll try," Mommy laughed, as the flakes continued to pour.

The Sweet Sky

Written by: Sara Weinberg and Makenna Susman

Illustrated by: Emelia Weir

Have you ever asked yourself why the sky is blue?

Did you know the sky is really a giant piece of candy you can chew

It's stretchy like taffy but melts in your mouth like a mint

Grownups simply cannot take a hint

I've heard that you can even get there by car,

50 thousand feet away but that is not too far

My neighbor ran all the way up to grab a snack

She sent me a postcard saying she was never coming back

Just one taste and you will know

You will never let this giant candy go

But for now, until you can make it there,

Be sure to get good dental care!

THANK YOU!

We trust that you have enjoyed this book and the message of hope behind it. By purchasing a copy, you have improved and deeply touched a homeless child's life. Please encourage your friends to do the same! Our dream is that these verses and illustrations will influence kids and grownups alike to use their voices to fight for the voiceless.

With Gratitude,

The Verses for the Voiceless Team

Illustrated by: Cassie Levy

41447477R00024

Made in the USA
San Bernardino, CA
04 July 2019